ADYNOMOSAURUS

AZHDARCHO

PROBACTROSAURUS

GENYODECTES

DACENTRURUS

MEGARAPTOR

MOABOSAURUS

IRRITATOR

NEBULASAURUS

TARBOSAURUS

JANE YOLEN

How Do Dinosaurs Say Goodbye?

Illustrated by
MARK TEAGUE

SCHOLASTIC PRESS • NEW YORK

Library of Congress Cataloging-in-Publication
Data available

ISBN 978-1-338-36335-7

10 9 8 7 6 5 4 3 2 1   21 22 23 24 25

Printed in China   38
First edition, October 2021

For Robbie, whose mom asked me to write a book
for him which began all the How Do Dinos books,
aka The Dinosty — J.Y.

To Bonnie — M.T.

How does a dinosaur say goodbye?

Does he shake his head hard?

Does she give a loud cry?

PROBACTROSAURUS

Does he hide in his bedroom,
an ache in his tummy,
the first day of school
'cause he won't see his mummy?

NEBULASAURUS

Does she stay in the girls' room,
her tears on the tile,
though the school nurse keeps trying
to get her to smile?

Or when Dad leaves for work
does she grab at his coat?
Or stick in his pocket
a very sad note?

When his parents go out
for a date at the mall,
does a dinosaur crayon
DON'T GO! on the wall?

When Grandma goes home again
after a stay,
does a dinosaur mess up
the guest room that day?

If Mom's in the hospital,
and Dad visits a bit,
does a dinosaur yell
at the girl come to sit?

MOABOSAURUS

Does a dinosaur run,
as their moving time nears,
down the street to the neighbors,
eyes streaming with tears?

No, dinosaurs don't —
they face their worst fears.

They tell all the grown-ups
just how they are feeling.
It helps right away
for fast dinosaur healing.

They give lots of hugs,
and they get lots back, too.
'Cause that's what each dinosaur

parent will do.

Then dinosaur kids
make a big paper heart.
They fill it with love
for the time they're apart.

They give goodbye kisses
and walk out the door.

Goodbye with a heart,

little dinosaur.

ADYNOMOSAURUS

AZHDARCHO

PROBACTROSAURUS

GENYODECTES

DACENTRURUS

MEGARAPTOR

MOABOSAURUS

IRRITATOR

NEBULASAURUS

TARBOSAURUS